Henry Naegely

The Mummer

And other poems

Henry Naegely

The Mummer
And other poems

ISBN/EAN: 9783337406516

Printed in Europe, USA, Canada, Australia, Japan

Cover: Foto ©Andreas Hilbeck / pixelio.de

More available books at **www.hansebooks.com**

THE MUMMER,

AND OTHER POEMS.

BY

HENRY GAËLYN,

LONDON :
ELLIOT STOCK, 62, PATERNOSTER ROW, E.C.
1895.

PREFACE.

WHEN I wrote 'The Mummer,' I was not aware that the conversion and martyrdom of St. Genesius, the comedian, formed the ground-plot on which Rotrou, the friend and precursor of 'le grand Corneille,' built one of his noblest tragedies.

His tragedy—a tragedy within a tragedy—has, however, little in common with the simple narrative as set forth in the 'Lives of the Saints,' and, indeed, the naïve pathos and the uncouth mediæval humour of the original would have been but little adapted to the stately style of his day.

The title of his play, 'St. Genest,' is misleading, as I find that St. Genest, or Genestius, was Bishop of Clermont-Ferrand, but Rotrou possibly adopted that orthography for the sake of euphony.

I know of no metrical version of the story in English, but this, I fear, may be a confession of culpable ignorance, as I can hardly suppose that I am the first to have been tempted by so striking a subject.

HENRY GAËLYN.

CONTENTS.

CONTENTS

THE MUMMER.

UNDER the low-born Diocletian's rule,
There dwelt in Rome a mummer, a court-fool,
Who, in his master's eyes to find more grace,
Pursued with hatred all the Christian race.
For that, or else because their simple rites,
Opposed to all fantastic lewd delights,
Were slowly gathering to their sober band
The wisest and the wealthiest in the land,
The very name of Christ would make him shake
With palsied anger. Martyrs at the stake,
Withering in flames, or weltering in their gore,
By wild beasts torn, were sights that he loved more
Than fairest pageants. Ever he would mock
With ape-like gibes the persecuted flock.

After much labour, the poor giddy clown,
Hoping to please the court and draw the town,
Devised, with some his peers, a ribald mime,
Tagg'd with mad jest and song to suit the time;
Just as upon the modern stage we see
The travesty of some old mystery.

As for the plot, it was not far to seek ;
For then, as now, among the strong some weak
Backsliders could be found ; and of his kin
Were sundry Christians, who his soul to win
Unto their ways, expounded doctrine clear
That was not lost on his attentive ear.
Upon the play-bills of that distant day
Thus ran the title of the scoffing play :
' The Holy Christian Chrismal Rite, this noon.
Genesius, author, convert, and buffoon.'

The house was crammed, the Emperor was there
Surrounded by the great, the rich, the fair ;
A glorious pageant, all that could surprise
And dazzle and enchant mere worldly eyes.
Gay gleams of sunlight ever flashed and played
Athwart the heavy awning's purple shade,
Sparkling upon a hundred diadems
Wrought in pure gold and precious orient gems,
Now flecking marble columns with their rays,
Now fainting midst the censer's odorous haze,
Now lingering on some Eastern beauty's cheek
Or playing with bright eyes at hide and seek,
Roving o'er scarlet, emerald, and blue,
And dying on sweet flowers of every hue.
Meanwhile low sounds of dulcimer and flute,
Murm'ring in cadence with the harp and lute,
Mingle with snatches of soft amorous song
Scarce heeded by the gay expectant throng.

Now all is husht, the gossip's tongue is still
That erst was clacking like a busy mill:
E'en whispering lovers hold their peace, and all
Are mute as statues in that mighty hall.

Padded, upon a couch, a monstrous size,
In mimic agony the mummer lies.
His groans and sighs provoke unending mirth,
While some about him pinch his mighty girth.
'Oh, take this fardel from me,' then he moans,
'Although ye leave me but my skin and bones!'
The doctors after consultation low
Answer, with many a solemn mock and mow,
'We are not joiners, skilless with the plane,
Our handiwork would hardly ease thy pain;
But here be Christian leeches who shall cure
Thy body with their nostrums. Ay, be sure
Not only shall their magic make thee whole,
But at the same time they will save thy soul.'

Now two attired in modest garb appear
And with sour mien and sober gait draw near—
A priest and an exorcist. Sinners gray,
Old scoffers well prepared their parts to play.
With uncouth antics and with jests profane
They drag the mummer from his bed of pain
And dip him in a well of water fair,
And then with holy oil anoint his hair.
This done, in linen garments pure and white
They clothe the chill'd and dripping neophyte.

But lo ! the wretch's eyes, unseal'd by grace,
Behold a wondrous light, throughout all space,
Space infinite, beyond all human dreams
It flows in mighty sun-eclipsing streams;
More bright than where on spotless mountain snow
The purest beams of morning gleam and glow—
The light that struck Saul blind upon the way
That goes towards Damascus. Its clear ray,
Impleach'd with passioning hues, cleaves through the veil
Of the dull firmament grown sere and pale,
And in its midst, with glory fimbriate,
He sees the Throne and all the awful state
Of the Most High. From orb to orb, he sees
The angels wafted as upon the breeze
The halcyon is borne. White wing'd they fly
Like flights of doves athwart the summer sky.
Or like rathe blossoms, the fair spring-time's pride,
Floating on gentle zephyrs far and wide.
From star to star they speed, each one intent
Upon a hallow'd errand, each one bent
Upon some work of mercy. By the gate
He sees the shining ones with palms who wait
For those who conquer in this mortal strife
And gain the guerdon of Eternal Life.
Meanwhile there bursts upon his ravished ear
A song of love that throbs from sphere to sphere,
A song of love that draws his yearning soul
Nearer and nearer to the glorious goal :

'Seal'd servant, come,
  Forwander'd but not lost.
  The heavenly host
Shall bring thee to thy home.

'In spite of Hell,
  And Death and that dark way
  Where thou dost stray,
With thee it shall be well.

'For thee, His light
  Now shines, thou who wert blind
  And couldst not find
His path in thy mirk night.

'He shall not fail
  Thee in thine hour of need;
  No broken reed
Is He.   Thou shalt prevail.

'Thy crown behold,
  More bright than earthly crowns;
  No monarch owns
A crown of such pure gold.

'The lilies fair
  With the sun's glory dight
  Are not so white
As these thy vestments are.

'Behold the road
　　Made ready for thy feet!
　　Behold thy seat
Prepared in His abode!

'Faint not nor fear,
　　Thine hour of bitterness
　　And sore distress
Shall be forgotten here!

'Here is thy place
　　Of rest—thy glorious home.
　　We wait. O come
And look upon His face!

'We wait. O come!'

And now the trembling mummer sees the roll
Of all his sins upon a dusky scroll;
An angel dips it in the flood, and lo,
The scroll is whiter far than driven snow.
Spotless and pure it shines before his eyes
While in faint echoes the sweet music dies.
The vision fades, he stands as dumb and still
As one bestraught, bereft of wits and will
He seems. Adown his foolish painted face
In grimy lines flow happy tears of grace,
Smirching with rouge and dye his garments white,
While his wild eye pursues the withering light.
A Pater Noster while amort he stands,
Clutching his choking throat with bloodless hands.

'This is great art,' say some, some sit amazed,
And others cry, ' The patch is surely crazed !'

He wakes and sees again the proud array,
The power, the pomp, the beauty, of his day.

All that once dazzled him is now but dross,
Poor sordid orts.   The Glory of the Cross
Outshines it all.   The Emperor meanwhile
Was charmed with the mad medley, but his smile
Turns quickly to a dark and ominous frown,
As bending low before him the poor clown
With faltering voice proclaims his soul's new birth :
Cleansed in the holy flood from stains of earth.
Then, overcoming all his fleshly fear,
He cries aloud, so that all there may hear ;
' Dread Sovereign, when but now I thought to mock
The Christian's God and all the Christian flock,
I heeded nought but our poor worldly day
And deem'd all things subservient to thy sway ;
But now I know a greater One ; on high
He sits enthroned beyond the farthest sky,
The bright stars do His bidding, in His hand
This earth is hardly as a grain of sand.
He is the Lord of love and truth and light.
O Monarch, how shalt thou withstand the might
Of the Almighty ?   At thy latest hour
What shall avail thy cohorts and thy power?

And ye, O Sages! what your wisdom? Mere
Dull guesses in the dark! When ye appear
Before the Omniscient, say, will ye still prate?
Go to, be humble ere it be too late!
And ye, O wealthy, all your hoarded gold,
Shall it redeem the birthright ye have sold
For this world's lusts? O people, He alone
For all our sins and strayings can atone!'
But now the Emperor, grown white with rage,
Glares at the wretched mummer on the stage.
' Have ye no muzzle for yon Christian hound?'
He cries; 'lay hands upon him, hale him bound
To some deep dungeon, spare not torments dire;
Hunger and thirst and stripes and flames of fire
Shall be his portion.'
                        But t'was all in vain,
Their bitter torture wrung no cry of pain
Nor even a murmur from his lips; so they
At last grew weary, and upon a day
They led him to his death. By some 'tis said
That when beneath the axe's stroke his head
Roll'd in the dust, there shone athwart the sky
A wondrous light. Sweet sounds of minstrelsy
Some thought they heard as his soul winged its way
To the fair realms of everlasting day.

'That land of such dear souls, that dear, dear land.'
SHAKESPEARE.

O ENGLAND! God hath given thee quiet years,
 And plenty, and great vantage, and wide sway;
 But now dark clouds are closing round thy way,
And all that love thee are beset with fears;
Dreading to see thee humbled and in tears,
 To hungry nations fallen an easy prey:
 Most lamentable in thy swift decay,
A laughing-stock where once thou hadst no peers.

Remember all thou holdest in thy hand,
 Be vigilant, be strong, spare not thy store,
 Nor yet with treacherous calms be thou beguiled!
 A foeman's foot upon thy virgin shore
 Would stamp thee ever as a thing defiled,
'O land of such dear souls, O dear, dear land

THE RISING TIDE.

WHEN slowly waking from its cradled sleep,
  Calm and unfurrow'd by the wild wind's wing,
  The tide creeps on like some strange living thing,
It lisps old runes and secrets of the deep.
Along the sands the curving ripples sweep,
  And round the clefts where weeping sea-flowers cling
  They sport with all the flotsam that they bring,
The worn-out playthings Ocean would not keep.
Dimpled all over with false fawning smiles,
  The flood now crescive woos the sunlit land
  And ever murmurs its low siren rede.
With fitful dalliance and weird cheating wiles
  It conquers all the strongholds of the strand,
  Till the stern cliffs defy its serpent-greed.

DESPONDENCY.

LIKE silver flashing 'neath the summer sun,
  The countless lances of the wild sea wave
  Give battle to the cliff and crumbling cave,
Untiring till the victory be won.
No power shall stay them till their work be done;
  Deep toned and myriad voiced they ever rave.
  Unswerving shall their serried cohorts brave
The rocks, until the sands of Time be run.
Casting aside the weakness of the world,
  Oh to be merged a moment in their life!
    To feel their strength, to join their fierce mad play!
Even against the flinty headlands hurl'd,
  To sink a victim in their glorious strife
    Were better than this halting by the way.

TURNER.

IIis life was sordid and his home was bare,
  And deathly silent, ruinous and dim ;
  Few friendly footsteps crossed that threshold grim,
It might have been the dwelling of despair.
IIis speech was rude, he was of those who dare
  To look with scorn upon the fleeting whim
  Of ever-changing Fashion. What to him
Were all the gauds for which the worldly care !
IIe sought with thorns to hedge about his dream
  And keep the foolish herd from his domain,
  Whence he could see long bygone summers glow
On mountain, valley, cataract and stream,
  Or watch the storm, or mark the rainbow grow,
  Or the slow shadows steal across the plain.

MILLET.

CHILD of the glebe, the primal curse he knew,
  'The ground shall bring forth thistles. Ay, and thou
  Shalt eat the herb o' the field.' The sweating brow,
Hunger and cold and drought and blighting dew,
The toil of those that delve and those that hew
  Or from deep wells draw water—tasks that bow
  The strongest necks : these things he knew and how
The paths of ease are trodden but by few.
Yet in great reverence God's earth he saw,
  Who saw the humble flower beside the way,
    And midst the clouds the sun's bright crown of gold.
Tried but unvanquished by the world's hard law
    He wrought in patience, like those craftsmen old
  Whose names and fames still live in this our day.

COROT.

ATHWART the trivial turmoil of the street,
  What songs came floating from the country-side,
  From bubbling brook and rushy river wide !
What happy auguries, what visions sweet,
Thronged round his humble cradle ! Zephyrs fleet
  Whisper'd of woods, where timid Dryads hide,
  Where gleaming streams amidst the sallows glide
And bright-haired Nymphs fly past on furtive feet.
And later, what fair dreams through all his days
  Follow'd his footsteps o'er the peaceful land
Or hover'd round him in the pleasant ways !
  Aurora woo'd him and by many a strand
He kept her tryst. Spell-dower'd by her rays
  The page he limned shall brave Time's ruthless hand.

DELACROIX.

A TITAN tortured by a soul-fed fire
Unquenchable in cold Castalian streams,
Writhing to seize the evanescent dreams
For ever fading from his fierce desire.
A great magician, in whose coffers slept
  Haroun Al Raschid's treasures.   His clear eyes
  Beheld great Phœbus throned amidst the skies,
And the drear hill-side where our Lady wept.
A master, heir to all the wide domain
  Of poets' visions, his brave spirit sped
With Dante through the realms of endless pain,
  And rode with Faustus through the midnight dread,
And stood with Hamlet in the graveyard dim,
And saw on high the broad-wing'd Seraphim.

THE SEA.

O Sea, how we have loved thee! Since the dim far days
  When from dark northern lands, like swallows on the
    wing,
  In the sun's track, the swift barks of the Viking king
Fared to the cadence of rude runes sung in thy praise,
Our bards have been thy high-priests. To their reso-
    nant lays
  The storm-wind winds its wild horn. Who again shall
    bring
  So fair a tribute to thee? Who again shall sing
In such clear tones the glory of thy wave-paved ways? •
Hast thou not been our strength in bitter times of need,
  Our noblest heritage? Shall we sit still and see
    Thy fair and broad demesne pass to an alien hand?
Shall we be converts to the mad short-sighted creed
  Of peddling party-mongers? To be strong and free
  As thy free wave, has been the glory of our land.

LOST SOULS.

I.

Why art thou pale, why tremble, O most dear
  And most desired ?   Forget the dread red maze
  Through which we wandered in these latter days !
To the mad prophet's voice lend not thine ear !
Could all their shed blood buy one pearly tear
  Dimming thy starry eyes ?   The thorny ways
  Are all gone o'er.   With songs of joy and praise
The nations hail our state.   What shouldst thou fear ?
Thou who wert dauntless till we reached the goal
  Nor ever fainted till the battle won.
    Shall thy proud heart quail doubting Fate's decree !
My love, O loveliest, like the glorious sun
Shall chase these grisly shadows from thy soul,
  O Love, my love shall be thy sanctuary.

II.

By Lethe's stream they sit with staring eyes,
  Dim captives of the irrevocable past,
  With Memory's stringent coils about them cast,
While baleful visions ever round them rise.

In vain they strain and strive, the wan wave flies
  Their eager lips ; then shuddering, all aghast,
  They cling together as the mocking blast
Goes laden with their sighs and dolorous cries.
Cries, prayers, and curses than their prayers less dire ;
  For thus they pray : ' O give us once again
One dreamless hour, even though Hell's fiercest fire
  Through all Eternity, Hell's gnawing pain
Should be its ransom !' But the avenging Ire
  Hears not. Their cries and prayers are all in vain.

TRIOLETS.

TO ELISE.

WOULD I could write for my Elise
  Trim triolets and tensons tender,
And send them by the passing breeze!
Would I could write for my Elise
Rhymes that might touch and tease and please
  And make her think upon the sender!
Would I could write for my Elise
  Trim triolets and tensons tender!

Sweets to the sweet! O honey-bees
  Go, pillage all the woodland bowers!
Go, plunder all the broider'd leas;
Sweets to the sweet! O honey-bees
Forget your hives, to my Elise
  Bring the sweet spoils of sweetest flowers!
Sweets to the sweet! O honey-bees
  Go, pillage all the woodland bowers!

In her fair garden my Elise
  Sits murmuring an ancient lay
Of lovers' woes and lovers' ease.
In her fair garden my Elise

Sings, and lest her sweet song should cease
  The bird is silent on the spray.
In her fair garden my Elise
  Sits murmuring an ancient lay.

The winter wind moans through the trees,
  No sweet bird sings, the fields are sere,
The flowers are dead, the waters freeze.
The winter wind moans through the trees;
But by the bower of my Elise
  The summer lingers all the year.
The winter wind moans through the trees,
  No sweet bird sings, the fields are sere.

AUTUMN.

DRIVEN past by Autumn's breath,
  Red leaves, black clouds, for ever flying,
Red as blood, as black as death.
Driven past by Autumn's breath
O'er the tilth and o'er the heath,
  Whilst the dear year lies a-dying.
Driven past by Autumn's breath,
  Red leaves, black clouds, for ever flying.

CHILDREN'S LAUGHTER.

LAUGHTER caused by no one's bane,
  Silvery chime of children's voices,
Laughter giving no one pain.
Laughter caused by no one's bane,
Listen, how it rings again
  The laugh, which my dull heart rejoices !
Laughter caused by no one's bane,
  Silvery chime of children's voices.

THE LOST PRESENCE.

How is it I no longer see thy face,
  O lost companion of the dear fled years ?
  Is it because mine eyes are dimmed with tears ?
How is it I no longer see thy face ?
Why didst thou vanish leaving not a trace,
  Thou who hadst skill to banish all my fears ?
How is it I no longer see thy face,
  O lost companion of the dear fled years ?

THE TULIP.

OUR poets all have praised those modest maids,
  The daisy and the violet. I would sing
Dame Tulip, orgulous in her rich brocades,
  The Lady Mayoress of the urban spring.

LAST BLOSSOMS.

LAST blossoms that untimely blow,
  Still blush and bloom to honour her,
  Till withering winter shall inter
Your bleaching leaves neath wreaths of snow !

1894.

WILD deeds are rife, inert, with dull dazed eyes
Some leaders stare upon the face of Fate,
While others, careless leeches, all too late
Prate of the throes in which the century dies.

1894.

ERIS the serpent bound
 Seeks to regain her ancient sway,
 And leagued with Chaos, glares upon her prey,
Fair Peace, the olive-crowned.

COUNSEL.

THESE things, O brothers, and others
  Were made to lurk in the shade;
Pale, dank, rank weeds in the dark wood,
  Flowers in the sunshiny glade.
Brothers, bring not to the light
Things that are born of the night.

THE VISIT.

Go, take your thuribles and take
  Of laurel wreaths a goodly store!
All your sleek words shall hardly slake
  His thirst for praise.   He'll still want more.

THE SECRET.

WHY do the flowers stare at me?   Do they know
  The secret, that I deem'd was only known
  To the far stars?   Shall their strown petals blown
Carry the tale abroad to friend and foe?

THE VISION.

IT comes amidst the midnight gloom,
I scarcely see and scarcely hear it,
I know not if I love or fear it.
It comes amidst the midnight gloom
And wanders all about the room
As seeking one to help or cheer it.
It comes amidst the midnight gloom,
I scarcely see and scarcely hear it.

It softly sings, the strangest things;
Would I could understand them rightly!
Its shadowy form is not unsightly.
It softly sings the strangest things
And then it spreads its dusky wings
And dances, if the moon shine brightly.
It softly sings the strangest things;
Would I could understand them rightly!

The vision of a vanish'd dream,
The long-lost song of hope and gladness,
Toned by the wither'd years to sadness.
The vision of a vanish'd dream,

The murmur of Time's weary stream,
   That goads despairing souls to madness.
The vision of a vanish'd dream,
   The long-lost song of hope and gladness.

Although at dawn it takes its flight,
   All day I hear its crazy singing,
   Like ghostly chimes for ever ringing.
Although at dawn it takes its flight,
I watch and wait until the night
   Shall come, its fitful presence bringing.
Although at dawn it takes its flight,
   All day I hear its crazy singing.

INVOCATION.

Rise from the sea, O my dream!
Ah, sooner or later rise!
Let me see thee as in the bygone days
Thou wert seen by mortal eyes!

I wander on and hope that I may meet
  Thy form divine, upon the moonlit strand,
Or find at least the imprint of thy feet
  Graved on the curving sand.

In caverns dim, carved by the craving wave,
  Where creatures strange, born of the deep, abide,
  I sit and watch the ever changing tide
What time the wild winds rave.

And when the morning mists desert the shore,
  Like veils asunder drawn, my sleepless eyes
  Are strained, to see amidst the azure skies
Those eyes that I adore.

The silver sails float o'er the silver main,
The seasons pass, the bright suns rise and set,
The future changes to the past, and yet
Thou comest not again.

Rise from the sea, O my dream !
Ah, sooner or later rise !
Let me see thee as in the bygone days
Thou wert seen by mortal eyes !

IN A CITY.

DIM grimy way
In the dull drear City,
Where never a ray
Of God's sun, through the livelong day
Pierces the pall of the murky sky,
To tell of pity
And hope, to those who live and die
Day by day,
In that grimy way.
Yet there,
By yon crazy stair,
Long years ago, Love stayed his flight.
There,
In the dusky light
Love shook his wings and all was bright
For two true souls—and they
Until this day
Have found that grimy way
A pathway of delight.

ON A NEGLECTED TOMBSTONE.

WHO was Belinda ?   I don't know,
  But from the aspect of her tomb,
  She was, at least so I presume,
Forgotten many years ago.

Ill-favoured was she, or a shrew,
  Or a poor soul by love bewrayed,
A beauty false, a beauty true,
  An aged matron or a maid ?

Her story's lost and in the land
  Her memory is faded quite ;
  Sunk in oblivion's frozen night,
Erased by Time's destroying hand.

But when I see the green grass grow,
And all the humble flowers that blow
About her grave, though I may err,
I think the spring-time thinks on her.

NOSTALGIA.

I SIT and dream amidst the baleful glare
  Of this drear city bleaching in the light.
  Sepulchral, sad, and ever ghastly white,
Its towers and fanes gleam in the burning air.

All day the dismal cypress turns her shade,
  All day the shrivell'd crickets in the sun
  Carp, while the wither'd lizards rustling run
O'er yon dry stones where once a fountain played.

All day the sterile unresponsive sea,
  Tideless and voiceless, sleeps beneath the sky,
  While on its bosom fainting breezes die,
Bereft of spells to set the spirit free.

From all the garden plots, the poison'd breath
  Of strange exotic flowers fills the air,
  Weird flowers of magic colours fair and rare,
Born to be garner'd for the crown of Death.

In all the meagre land no song of birds,
　No blithesome carols in the early dawn,
　No dewdrops broidering the jaded lawn,
No bleat of lambs or sound of lowing herds.

No peace the twilight brings, no rest the night,
　Or broken slumbers haunted by fair dreams
　Of moors and mountains, lakes and crystal streams,
Bright visions fading with the morning light.

ENGLAND AND SWITZERLAND.

OUR Wordsworth sang in days gone by
Of that fair goddess Liberty,
   And how she found a home
Where Alpine summits pierce the sky,
Where eagles hardly dare to fly,
   And how she loved the foam ;

The foam that like a silver band
Encircles our dear native land,
   Not whiter than her feet.
And how, when from her fastness she
Was driven, by our Northern sea
   She found a sure retreat.

I too have seen her in my dream
Pass smiling by the mountain stream
   With Alpine roses crown'd.
I too have met her where the wave
Goes echoing through the Ocean cave
   In tumult of wild sound.

With Peace she walketh hand in hand,
And Truth and Justice near her stand
　　Whene'er she sits in state;
And if at times she wield the glaive,
Her arm is also strong to save,
　　Her love more strong than Fate.

About her robes the children cling,
About her paths the free birds sing,
　　About her paths of light.
Before the glance of her clear eyes,
More clear, more bright than morning skies,
　　All things of night take flight.

To mask wild deeds of blood and shame
Some seek to use her sacred name.
　　We know her hands are pure.
Some, following a mad fen flame,
Sink whelm'd in sloughs.　Is she to blame
　　Whose ways are always sure?

Some, purblind, see a spectre where
She sits, that goddess kind and fair.
　　May Heaven mend their sight!
Some try with spiders' threads to bind
Her wings.　Poor fools!　The strong North Wind
　　Would quail before her might.

O Liberty! O Liberty!
England hath been thy sanctuary
  And Switzerland thy throne.
And thou hast been our beacon bright,
The star that led us through the night
  O'er trackless ways unknown.

ELEGY.

FAME sought him not, he sought not Fame. His days
  Were passed in humble service at the shrine
  Of our great Mother, seeking truth Divine
Far from all beaten ways.

Careless of every gaud and empty toy,
  Heedless of vanities, he lived apart,
  Deaf to the turmoil, calm and true of heart
In sorrow and in joy.

The waving corn, the murmuring forest trees,
  Whisper'd to him of some great otherwhere ;
  While strains from a lost world still young and fair
Sang in the passing breeze.

Still young and fair, the world of poets' dreams
  Re-lived for him. Pan was not dead, his reeds
  Were vocal still and charmed the flowery meads
And naiad-haunted streams.

Here on the hillside it is therefore meet
  That in this copse-screen'd grave-garth he should lie,
  In peace beneath the ever-changing sky
'Mid fields and orchards sweet.

A humble plot that in the garish day
  Holds nought that you would notice as you pass,
  Except the simple flowers and waving grass
About the tombstones gray.

But when the night descends upon the plains
  And every bird hath gone unto his nest,
Save only Philomel, who still complains
  Of Love and Love's unrest;

Then stealing through the groves and moonlit glades
  The Nymphs and Dryads, those of Ceres' band,
And those who ever dwell in forest shades,
  Come hither hand in hand.

They circle round his tomb and chaunt a hymn
  Whose sweet accords are borne upon the breeze
  And mingling with the murmur of the trees
Float o'er the champaign dim.

Off'rings they bring, off'rings from Flora's wreath,
  Pomona's wealth and golden ears of corn,
Milk from the byre, and honey from the heath,
  White wool from yearlings shorn.

But ere the opal lights of morning gleam
  Between the sombre branches of the firs,
  And ere the lark amid the clover stirs,
They vanish like a dream.

THE SONG OF GOLD.

I FLEW to the top of a lone bare tree,
And I sang as loud as loud might be
In praise of the Lord of the land and the sea.

And the sun went up, and the sun went down,
And all the folk came out of the town
The man and the maid and the king with his crown.

And they sat them down on the drear dark hill,
Every Jack by the side of his Jill,
And the tongues of the wither'd old women were still.

And I sang and I sang till all was at rest,
Till the callow bird was asleep in the nest,
And the babe was husht on its mother's breast.

I sang of the Lord of the land and the sea
Before whose throne all bow the knee,
The rich and the poor and the bond and the free.

Of the Lord of the world, of the red, red gold,
That rejoices the hearts of young and old
And makes weak men strong and cowards bold.

Of gold, the master of king and slave,
For which sages toil and scheme and save;
The one good thing for which all men crave.

And of how they knew no unhappiness
Who worship'd that god, and no distress,
Nor aught of the world's unkindliness.

And I sang, 'Bow down in the dust and pray
That his shining eyes may look your way
And ye too may be happy in this your day.'

But one arose and in accents clear
That echo'd about the hillside drear
Cried aloud so that even the deaf might hear :

'O my friends, beware of that fatal rede,
Of the baleful song of gold and greed,
But heed my words, for great is your need !

'O great is your peril, the passing bell
Were less dread to hear than that song of Hell
Which for many fair souls has toll'd the knell !

'For gold is the lord of an empire dire
For whose sake men risk eternal fire,
'Tis the fee of shame and the murderer's hire.

'Ay, gold is the price of the widow's moan,
Of the orphan's wail.   More hard than stone
Is the heart that is set upon gold alone.

' O'er the sea and the land gold's power is great,
But it turns not aside the hand of Fate
Nor serves to pay toll at heaven's gate.'

As he spoke, the folk swayed to and fro,
And some arose as though fain to go
To their peaceful homes, but their feet were slow.

Slow and heavy as lead, and their gaze
Was as wild as the gaze of one who strays
In the midnight drear o'er haunted ways.

But a caitiff wretch crept near and drew
His sword and slew the prophet true,
And the thirsty earth drank his blood like dew.

Then each one started as who should see
In Fate's dark glass his destiny
And rises up to turn and flee.

In tumult wild, like a savage horde
Adown the hillside bare they poured,
And the corpse lay stark on the blood-stained sward.

Ay, goaded and crazed by my song of sin,
With hideous clangour and fiendish din,
Through the city gates they all rush'd in.

And the sun set red and the night's black shroud
Fell o'er dome and temple and palace proud
And the tocsin bell rang clear and loud.

And all was laid waste by sword and fire,
Brother slew brother and son slew sire,
And the whole town blazed like a funeral pyre.

And thousands were flying and thousands had fled,
And thousands were dying and thousands were dead,
And the conduits and kennels with blood ran red.

At dawn but a heap of ashes lay there
Where once arose that city fair,
And a pall of smoke swayed aloft in the air.

Years after, as over that land I flew,
I marked in my flight that no green thing grew
Save the cypress sad and the dismal yew.

Yet there on the hill, in the very place
Where the martyr's blood had left a trace,
Grew one sweet herb—'the Herb of Grace.'

A FABLE.

THE patient spider all the morn had spun
While gilded flies were dancing in the sun.
But ere the sultry noonday hours were past,
The earth with low'ring clouds was overcast,
The trembling trees proclaimed the tempest nigh,
And soon the lightning rent the pitchy sky,
While howling gusts and hail and splashing rains
Destroyed the work of so much toil and pains.
Had she not found a providential lair,
Arachne's days had surely ended there.
Meanwhile in nooks and crannies snug and warm
The flies slept heedless of the raging storm.

Moral.

Let us be happy in the sun, nor waste our time, and wit,
    and labour,
In setting traps for other folks and scheming how to
    catch our neighbour.

THE SINGERS.

MAN sings but of the things he loves or hates; the song
   Of Love shall surely ever ring the clearest;
   The sweetest song shall be of what is dearest.
Yet scorn and noble hate, the scorn and hate of wrong
Have also struck true chords and deep-toned on the lyre.
     In every time and clime,
     The folly and the crime
Of man, have waked the prophet's and the poet's ire.
These are the broad-wing'd ones, who sear with words of
   fire
All human frailty; mighty seers who see
God's awful judgments, knowing no dulcet harmony
Of pastoral pipes, to gather in the flocks that stray
Or cheer the palmer on the rugged way.

Elliot Stock, 62, Paternoster Row London.